W9-BVB-446

Discard
NHCPL

Triad Hauntings

Burt Calloway   Jennifer FitzSimons

Cover Art: Gray Erlacher
Photography: Gray Erlacher and Jennifer FitzSimons

BANDIT
BOOKS

Winston-Salem, North Carolina

LIBRARY OF CONGRESS CATALOG CARD NUMBER 90-83941
ISBN 1-878177-00-1
BANDIT BOOKS
P.O. BOX 11721
WINSTON-SALEM, NORTH CAROLINA 27106
TYPESET AT NEWSOUTH PRINTING, INC., WINSTON-SALEM, NC
PRINTED IN THE UNITED STATES OF AMERICA

To Millie Erlacher, whose living spirit is a joy for all who know her.

Contents

Foreword

The communities in and around Greensboro, High Point, and Winston-Salem are rich in folklore, as we discovered when researching this book. This is normal for such a long established and populous area. Ghost stories have long been favorites among almost everyone around the world. It's only natural that the Triad of North Carolina should have its share of these tales. Even the hallowed halls of the Executive Mansion in Raleigh are apparently blessed with the spirit of a nineteenth-century governor.

The best part of the research was meeting and interviewing dozens of people from all walks of life. This delightful group included doctors, sales people, housewives, bank vice-presidents, social workers, and people of many other occupations, proving that a spirit can touch the life of anyone. There is no particular type of character or personality that appears to be immune to the manifestations of a determined ghost.

Unfortunately, we were not able to use all the stories we were told. As the book went to press, the phone was still ringing with folks calling who had just heard about our research and were offering to tell of their experiences. We found that a volume of books would be necessary to publish all the ghost stories from the Triad Area, and another volume is in the planning. We also heard of countless adventures that took place in other parts of the state or country. Contrary to what many believe, there is no shortage of ghostly encounters.

Thank you to all those people who took the time to pass on their stories. For the ones that were printed, some of the contributors allowed us to use their real names, while others asked that we keep them anonymous. We've done our best to respect those wishes.

Thank you to all the employees of the local newspapers, radio stations, libraries, police and sheriffs' departments, and historical societies who have helped us along the way. The questions that these people answered must have seemed strange at the time, but they were invaluable in gathering information.

Some people believe in ghosts, some don't. Most of the unbelievers will admit to the possession of some curiosity about the subject. Whatever your beliefs, we hope you will enjoy reading about the encounters of your friends and neighbors.

Happy hauntings.

The Night of Terror

THERE IS A HOUSE in Stokes County that we heard about repeatedly during our research for this book. It is well-known to local inhabitants and teenagers. Located on a lonely area of Payne Road, the house and surrounding grounds have a mysterious aura. This was the scene of the tragic shooting death of a young woman a few years ago. Unwanted visitors have vandalized the house, leaving it in poor condition, and the owners are understandably upset about trespassers.

Each person interviewed seemed to know a different tale about the area, about how this or that happened to a friend. The recurring story involves a bridge located a short distance from the house. If a car stops on the bridge and the engine is turned off, it will not restart. Then if one looks over into the woods, he sees a ghost, the body of a man hanging from a rope around the limb of a huge tree.

One young woman related her own experience at the house on the condition that she remain anonymous, so we'll call her Cathy.

A few years ago when Cathy was a teenager, a date named Gilbert drove her over to the area around eleven o'clock on a Saturday night. He stopped the car squarely in the center of the bridge that they had heard was haunted, and, throwing out his chest, told her bravely that he would protect her from the

1

demons near the bridge that would prevent the car from starting again. She wasn't impressed because, as she put it, "His car was a beat-up Duster with 'bout a million miles on it, and the thing didn't start half the time anyway." To further demonstrate his strength and fearlessness, Gilbert got out of the car and walked around on the bridge. Then he strutted over to the woods and dared any spooks to come and get him.

Cathy was beginning to feel "a little creepy" and was wishing Gilbert would come back and take her away from there. The spring weather was uncomfortably warm and a thunderstorm was blowing up, with black clouds gathering and blotting out the moon. This made the night blacker and even more scary, and when the first flash of lightning ripped through the darkness, she jumped. Her heart was pounding and for just a second she felt relieved that her date was so gallant. Then she spotted him stumbling back toward the car "with the palest face and biggest bug-eyes" she had ever seen. He collapsed into the seat beside her and sat staring blankly. She screamed, "What was it? What'd you see?"

He opened his mouth but no sound came out. When she touched his shoulder he uttered, "Gh-gh-gh-ghost! The lightning ... It was ..."

"Never mind," Cathy yelled. "Get me out of here! Now! Hurry! Go!"

It crossed her mind that he might be playing a joke on her, but when he reached down and turned the key to start the car, his trembling hands assured her that he was serious. The engine turned over slowly, as if the battery was almost dead, and refused to start. Gilbert was shaking. The sound of his chattering teeth filled the car. They were stuck there on the bridge, with something ominous outside the car.

Gilbert seemed unable to move and just sat there, staring at the dashboard. Realizing it was up to her, Cathy jerked him out of the way, climbed over him to the driver's side, and tried to start the car herself. Another flash of lightning made her think about the end of the world as the motor cranked and

House on Payne Road

cranked. Never had she silently prayed so hard or cursed so loudly as at that moment when the motor turned over more slowly each time. Just when she thought the battery had died, the engine fired. It sputtered for a moment and she fought not to let it go dead. A loud pop echoed around them. It could have been a backfire or a gunshot. Cathy didn't care what it was, she just rammed the car into gear and took off. She kept her eyes straight ahead, afraid to look out either side of the car. They barreled down the dirt road, sliding dangerously around each curve. At the very instant she felt they would escape, the hood flew up and crashed back against the windshield. Now completely blind to the road ahead of them, Cathy slammed on the brakes and prayed they would stop before hitting something. They skidded for what seemed an eternity before they went off into the ditch and stopped abruptly. It was a minute before she realized they were still alive. The engine had died again.

Cathy looked over at Gilbert, whose pale face seemed to glow in the dark, and asked if he was all right. Gilbert

3

answered in a squeaky voice that he was. Cathy said, "Well, don't just sit there. Get out and put the hood down so we can get out of here."

Gilbert squirmed and said, "I would, but I sprained my ankle back there. I don't think I can walk."

"Can't you hop up there on one foot?"

"No, I better not. Something might be broken, it's hard to tell. You go put it down."

"Me? I'm not going out there! You do it, you're the boy."

Gilbert replied, "Well, you're driving." So they sat there in the car and listened to the thunder growing in intensity. Gilbert moaned and rubbed his ankle a few times, although Cathy was sure he wasn't rubbing the same ankle each time.

Gilbert then described what he had seen back at the bridge as a face in the trees, frightening Cathy even more. The woods on either side of the road looked dark and menacing, and several times when the lightning lit up the night both of them swore they saw something watching them. Every noise from outside the car sounded like the arrival of death to them. Despite the heat, they rolled up the windows and locked the doors. They argued repeatedly about who should get out, but neither one would give in. So they ended up spending the night right there in the car, sitting in the ditch with the hood up. "What a great night," Cathy said, "sitting in the car with that loser, sweating like a pig, and scared out of my skin about something that may or may not have ever been there."

Their courage was reborn with the light of morning and they both got out, put the hood down, and went home. Cathy noticed Gilbert wasn't even limping that morning. Her parents, refusing to believe her story, grounded her for six months since she had only recently been allowed to date and had already started abusing the privilege. The sentence was later reduced to three weeks. By threatening to tell of Gilbert's cowardice, she was able to keep the secret of that night between the two of them, as far as she knows.

Cathy's story ended there. She told us about how the

house had fallen victim to the ravages of vandals over the years. She feels a spooky old house and grounds will always be associated with a scary ghost tale. It's human nature.

TOP: The Thompson House;
BOTTOM: Mr. Thompson's path and entrance into the washroom

The Ghost Trying to Get Home: The Thompson House

IN THE MID-NINETEEN THIRTIES, John Thompson worked as a carpenter in Winston-Salem. He was the father of four, a hard worker, and a man of routine. Every night, he'd walk home, swing open the weighted gate, and walk around to the basement door to wash his hands before walking upstairs to eat dinner with his wife and children.

One cold January night in 1937, he was never to make it home. He stopped by the store on his way home to pick up some groceries for his wife. With a bag of groceries in his arm, he made his way down Acadia Street to a point between Freeman and Holton Streets, just opposite the two-story house he lived in. Without looking, he began to cross the road. As he did, he stepped into the path of a car driven recklessly by a neighbor, who did not throw on the brakes in time to prevent the car from hitting Thompson, leaving him lying in the street with a fractured skull.

As John lay unconscious on the cold pavement, many of his neighbors came out to assist him with blankets and bandages. His wife and youngest daughter sobbed beside him, and tried to comfort him, but he had been rendered unconscious as soon as the car struck. He was taken to Baptist Hospital, but it was to no avail. He never regained consciousness.

Apparently, it was so unexpected that his spirit never accepted his death.

Ten years later, a young newlywed couple, Ann and Sam Bobbit, rented two rooms of the Thompson house. One of their windows looked out on the path Mr. Thompson had taken daily around the back of the house to the basement to wash his hands.

One night when her husband was out, Ann was listening to the Hit Parade when she heard a squeak, like the gate swinging open. Assuming that her husband was coming home, she eagerly jumped up and ran downstairs to meet him, only to find the yard dark and empty.

"Sam? You home Sam?" she called.

There was no answer, so she went back upstairs to her radio show. Her favorite song came on, and she was singing along with the chorus when she heard the gate open again. Quickly she turned down the volume on the radio and listened. She heard heavy footsteps on a hard surface, shuffling and stepping, shuffling and stepping, sounding as if the soles were scratching sand. Then Ann listened as the hinges of the basement door squeaked and a faucet was opened, letting water splash out into a basin for a time, then the faucet was turned off. She opened the upstairs door to the basement and called to Mrs. Thompson, hoping that her landlady would answer her.

None of this made sense to her, because ever since she had lived there, the faucet in the basement had been inoperable. As a matter of fact, nobody came around to the backdoor from that direction. Also the ground had been wet for days and the footfalls sounded as if they were on a decidedly dry surface, like a sidewalk. And there wasn't even a sidewalk on that side of the house!

Soon her husband came home, complaining about the tire on his car going flat. Luckily it had happened close enough to home that he managed to get the car into the driveway. Ann told him about the noises she had heard:

"It happened twice. The first time I thought it was you," she said. "Then the second time, whoever it was ran the faucet downstairs."

"Well, maybe Mrs. Thompson got that faucet down there working while we were out."

"She ain't home, Sam."

"Well, it's probably nothing."

Later that evening, Sam went to the back corner of the house where he'd left his car, to change the flat tire so he wouldn't have to do it the next morning before he went to work. Ann followed him downstairs to talk to him as he worked. Sam was complaining about the wet ground when Ann held up her hand to silence him: "Shhhh. Listen!"

This time they both heard it, the long squeak of the gate, which they could see was not opening, and the steady gritty, shuffling footfalls of heavy shoes walking toward them on the wet grass.

Ann let go of Sam's arm and backed up against the hedge to let whatever it was pass. Sam stood up and remained dead still in his tracks, stunned. As steps approached him, he began to feel chilled. He swallowed to keep his pounding heart out of his throat. Suddenly the steps were behind him, continuing on to the back door. He felt the chill subside. They listened to the sound of the back door opening and the faucet running.

"When is our lease up?" asked Sam.

The next day they went down to talk to Mrs. Thompson about moving.

"You must have heard," the woman said solemnly.

"Heard what?" Sam asked.

"John trying to get home." She looked at the ground. "He was killed on his way home, and now he still tries to come home for dinner. It's just like when he was returning from work. Sometimes there are long periods when nothing is heard of him at all, and then, all of a sudden, he'll try again several times in one night. I can tell you one thing, though, he means no harm. It's all a little sad."

Ann and Sam decided not to move out. They stayed on for two years, growing accustomed to the occasional footsteps outside their window.

The next occupant, Gloria Caines, talked about hearing the footsteps at night.

The gate and the hedge are gone now. The side of the house where Mr. Thompson was heard isn't recognizable as a walkway at all. At some point in the last forty years a fish pond was installed out there. The house now has new siding and appears quite different than it was in the forties, but Sam and Ann's daughter, Jane Saylor, says that Thompson's footsteps can still be heard.

The house has just been purchased by a delightful woman, Jeanette Wells, who is running a boarding house there. She admits that she is afraid of ghosts and doesn't want to have Mr. Thompson spooking around her house.

Darius Williamson, one of Well's boarders, has had a hair-raising experience. He says that one day while he was resting, something pinched his calf, startling him. He was alone in the house at the time, but told Mrs. Wells about it when she returned home, before they knew anything about Mr. Thompson. Neither of them have yet heard the footsteps.

Perhaps Mr. Thompson is just in another dormant period before he tries to come home again, or perhaps he has finally made it into the house.

The Poltergeist by the Church

FIFTEEN YEARS AGO Buddy Shelton was what one might call a rounder. He hitchhiked through all of the South, including North Carolina, looking for adventure and supporting himself here and there by odd house painting and construction jobs. I met him two years ago in Chapel Hill when I first became interested in recording ghost stories of that area. Although he was sporting a suit and tie when I met him, I could tell that at one time he had been quite a free spirit, full of color and bravado. When I told him about my interest in ghost stories, he gave me an account of his only run-in with the ghostly world, and it took place in Forsyth County.

"I don't know much about ghosts," he said, "but I know one area around Winston-Salem that I will never go through again."

Buddy said he had picked up some construction work around Winston-Salem for a few months in the mid-seventies, and one night he was trying to hitch a ride to Kernersville, where a girl he had met lived. He said that he was walking down Glen "something" Road when he got to the corner where a church was. He had been this way before and knew to take the road that went down beside the church to 150.

He stopped in front of the church to have a rest and ate a package of cheese and crackers that he had bought. He sat

11

quietly enjoying the spring breeze rustling the trees above him. The cooler air made him wonder if it was going to rain, but when he looked up he saw the sky filled with stars.

It was late. There were some houses across the street, but all of their lights were out. Feeling rather alone, Buddy stood up and began walking down the road beside the church. He heard a car coming, and stuck out his thumb. The car passed him by. The next thing he knew, something shoved him hard onto the ground. He got up and looked around, expecting to find someone who had sneaked up from behind him. There was nobody there. Just the dim T-shaped junction of the two roads, and the sleeping houses beyond. Around him the chirps of crickets reached a crescendo, and a shiver went down his spine. He no longer felt like he was truly alone.

He turned and continued walking, with all of his senses tuned into his environment. He decided he must have just lost his footing somehow and fell, and that he had only imagined being pushed. He was tired. It had been a long day. He took a step or two more, feeling slightly more at ease, and then, BAM! It happened again. Whatever this thing was, it could really land a punch. Suddenly he was aware of a weird, tingling feeling, like electricity traveling from his right shoulder, down his arm, and out his hand. All of the hair on that arm was standing on end. Buddy Shelton had never been so frightened in his whole life.

He stood back up and noticed a swirl of leaves not far away. It was a breezy evening, but the vortex of leaves, and the graveyard he was suddenly passing, made him think *ghost*. Then he heard a squeal and felt a pinch, and, at that instant, as he put it, "my ass was out of there."

He began running at a good clip, having no idea how long he would have to run before he could lose this beastly thing. At one point, he was sure it was still following him, although he couldn't hear it.

After running for what seemed like a half hour, but was probably just a few minutes, he heard a car coming. Feeling

with every bone in his body that this was the only chance he had, he suddenly found himself out in the middle of the road like a fool, trying to flag it down. It was an old guy in a truck. "He must have thought I was in deep trouble," Buddy said, "because he stopped."

"Let me in," Buddy yelled through the open window on the passenger side. "Something's trying to kill me." Before the old man could come to a complete stop, Buddy had the door open and was climbing in the front seat.

The driver allowed him to stay, and Buddy rode on to Kernersville with him, white as a ghost, his heart pounding.

Shelton said if he had been drinking that night, he would have written the whole incident off as an hallucination, but that he hadn't been drinking at all, because he didn't have any money.

Mr. Shelton left me with the impression that this was a turning point in his life. He said that after this experience, he never went out again at night. He also stopped drinking and started going to church on a regular basis. Sure enough, I met him at a church gathering.

When I did the research for this book I was surprised to find another odd occurrence that seems to have happened in this same area. W.K. McNeil wrote a book called *Ghost Stories from the American South.* In this book there is the brief story of W.T. Dollar, who worked as a tobacco drummer for R.J. Reynolds. Although White Top and Konnarock are mentioned as places Dollar passed, and are not in this area as far as I know, (the author also thought Gold Hills was in Eastern Forsyth County) there are some striking geographical coincidences.

It seems that around 1919, Dollar was riding his horse home from work one night when the horse stopped suddenly, refusing to budge, and a presence got on the horse with him, and sat behind the saddle.

When Dollar got to Oak Grove Baptist Church, the horse stopped again, and whatever it was dismounted. The horse continued by Elliot's Garage, which, the author points out, is no longer there, and on to his house behind the garage.

When Mr. Dollar got home, he saw white streaks on the horse's flanks. He was very frightened by the whole experience and never traveled this way at night again.

This could very likely be the same church that Mr. Shelton talked about. He spoke of a road called Glen "something" Road intersecting a road that eventually ran into 150. Glenn High Road intersects Oak Grove Road which runs to 150. At the junction of these two roads sits Glenn View Baptist Church, formerly Oak Grove Baptist, which is the church McNeil writes that W.T. Dollar rode by. Behind the church, on Oak Grove Road, is a graveyard. If these two stories share the same location, then Shelton was walking up Oak Grove Road at the time of his attack.

Now there is a new development of homes along this part of Oak Grove Road and it all looks very new and safe, but if there is any truth to these stories, then let he who travels here after dark beware. An angry spirit with exceptional powers lurks in the area.

Phantom of Dana Auditorium

DANA AUDITORIUM has been known for its haunts for more than forty years, ever since it was built. The beautiful brick structure occupies the area believed to have been the location of a field hospital during the Battle of Guilford Courthouse, during the Revolutionary War. As such, it was undoubtedly the scene of much suffering and death.

Perhaps this hospital was the origin of Dana's renowned ghost, Lucas, who occasionally accompanies security guards on their nightly rounds through the building.

One of the former security guards at Guilford College told us that he himself has never had a run-in with Lucas, but that many of the guards who routinely patrol the place have.

The ghost or ghosts (a few people believe there is more than one!) seem to be active in two rooms: the Moon Room and the Choir Room.

The guards often hear Lucas playing the piano in the Choir Room. There are quite a few pianos in there, but Lucas prefers tickling the ivories of the piano located on a slightly elevated platform. The guards can hear the music as they approach the door to the Choir Room, but when they enter the room, the piano becomes silent.

Guards have also spotted an illuminated window in either the Moon Room or the Choir Room from outside the building, gone in, and found the light in that room turned off. Or else, they have turned off the light and then seen it burning again, once they were back outside.

One night seventeen years ago, two security guards at Guilford College walked into Dana Auditorium on a routine check. They were known as Freak and Straight, because one was a long-haired hippie and the other was a clean-shaven veteran. Freak happened to be standing on the stage, and Straight, in the first row of seats, when they heard, "Swoosh. Swoosh." They looked above them and watched one of the four large crystal chandeliers overhead swinging rhythmically back and forth, gaining momentum. They couldn't figure out what was propelling the huge light fixture. They were alone in the building. There was no open window to provide a breeze. Freak and Straight then watched in terror and amazement as the chandelier broke away from the ceiling and fell to the rows of chairs below, shattering upon impact. As legend has it, Freak's first reaction was, "Far out man. Let's do'em all."

Another time a guard who did not believe in ghosts at all and had scoffed at the alleged ghostly incidents in Dana, was walking out of the Moon Room, preparing to lock up for the night. As he rounded the corner he saw the figure of a man in front of him. All he could make out was that the man was wearing a weathered hat pulled down low on his head.

"Hey, this is Guilford Security. Can you tell me what you are doing here?" the guard asked.

The man didn't answer. The guard called to him again. At this time the man looked toward him, then turned and walked through the wall to the guard's left, which led into the Moon Room. The guard ran out of the building in fear. Very shaken, yet still skeptical about what he had seen, he told the head of security about it the next day.

Another security guard, Marcus, says that he was locking up Dana one night when he felt something following him. It stopped where he stopped, and continued along after him

Dana Auditorium

when he walked on. He felt it strongest in the Choir Room. It disappeared when he went upstairs, but when he descended it continued following him. He said he can't describe exactly what it was, except he knew that he wasn't alone. His body felt a cold, yet tingly sensation, which could have been fear, although he described it as feeling almost like some kind of electrical current.

Another time when Marcus was locking up one of the exit doors in the main auditorium, he was unable to pull the door completely shut. It felt as if someone was pulling the door in the opposite direction. He then went outside, saw nobody, and tried to shut the door. It clicked shut without any hesitation.

A theater student who was working in Dana late one night reported seeing the transparent figure of a person just sitting in the balcony. She said that she watched it for some time until it gradually faded to nothing.

One odd coincidence concerning all of these events in that they happened around two o'clock in the morning.

Perhaps Lucas was a soldier who died in the field hospital

in the late eighteenth century, and never found his way beyond the aimless world of specters. Now he wanders the halls of some strange building, erected around him much later. Well, at least he's been out of the cold for forty years.

The Ghost that Flew the Coop

THERE'S NOT MUCH HAPPENING at 909 Church Street these days, but for about seventy years, up until 1969, the ghost of a little old Moravian lady kept occupants on their toes with her antics.

Stu Whitworth was one of them. He moved there in the mid-sixties ahead of his wife, Sandy, and their new baby boy, Blair, to prepare the house for them. The house needed some interior work, and he planned on doing some minor repairs, painting, and re-hanging all the doors, which were, for some reason, removed and stacked in the attic. Only the bathroom door was left in place. Yet, even with all this work ahead of him, Stu was very happy to have found such a nice roomy house in picturesque Old Salem.

One night he was painting the walls in the bathroom, when he heard a knock on the bathroom door. He climbed down off the ladder and opened the door. Nothing was there. An eerie silence rang in his ears for a moment, but he decided it was just his imagination and went back to work. Then there was another knock at the door, only this time the sound was sharper and louder, more like a kick than a knock. Stu could feel the pressure of the knock in the bathroom. He opened the door again, but nobody was there. He decided to just dismiss the whole thing, still feeling lucky to have found the house, and that he wasn't about to spoil it with paranoia and fear. Something must have fallen, and that was that.

Like most people, Stu hesitated to believe in the supernatural. He had a college education, and he was a skeptic.

The next night he returned home from work and found the screen door latched from the inside, even though there was nobody in the house who could have done this.

Then things got worse. These episodes took on almost poltergeistic elements. Doors began to open and slam upstairs. Lights went off in the room where Stu was painting and came on in other rooms. The radio station kept switching from his station to a station playing classical music.

Stu got fed up with painting (and possibly a bit spooked) and called a painter to finish the job.

The first day the painter worked there, he couldn't get the lights on, so he checked the fuse box. While he was looking at the fuses, the lights came on.

So he started painting. The lights remained on. His mind drifted, then snapped back to attention when he heard the undeniable sound of tapping on glass. He figured Stu was outside trying to get his attention. He looked through all the windows, but didn't see him. Then he noticed something weird. There were screens on the outside of the windows. Therefore, anyone tapping on the glass had to do so from the inside of the window. The tapping continued, but he had a job to do, so he turned on the radio hoping the music would stop the noise from distracting him. Then the station changed to a funeral march.

The painter was thoroughly frazzled by this time. He decided to leave. Just as he was getting his things together, he saw a shadow and became so frightened, he jumped through the screen door.

Sandy and Baby Blair soon arrived, all ready to settle into their new home, but the ghost continued its playful capers: footsteps were still heard along with tapping on the windows. Lights went on and off, and the radio stations kept changing.

House on Church Street

All of this seemed to be an effort to get attention from the living occupants. Undoubtedly the ghost had that.

Then one day, by chance, Stu met the previous occupant who, Stu was glad to know, was already familiar with the ghost. Stu found out that it was this man who had taken all the interior doors off their hinges, because something kept slamming them.

Stu soon decided to enlist the help of a psychic, a woman from New York. He invited her over to see what she could tell him about the situation.

As soon as she entered the house she could feel a presence. The ghost sensed her power, and perhaps didn't trust her, because when the psychic went into the playroom she felt a sudden jolt.

The psychic then meditated for a while, and informed the couple that the ghost was a little old woman with laced up boots and a cane, hence the tapping. She said that the woman had been stuck in the "astral world" for seventy years, and that she was lonely. She also said that she was the first person with whom the ghost had communicated in all that time.

The next night the psychic was eating at another person's house and noticed that the ghost from Church Street was still with her. The psychic later told Stu that she had invited the ghost back to New York with her to meet other inhabitants of the spirit world, and the ghost had taken her up on it. After that, nothing more was ever heard of the ghost at 909 Church Street.

I spoke with a woman currently working at the address, and she said that the place is still quiet. One hopes that the spirit of the little old lady found some other spirits to keep her company in New York, or maybe she found her way beyond the astral world to the world of peace.

Odors, Eyeballs, and Footsteps

IN THE SUMMER of 1957, the Wagoner family rented a house on U.S. 311 in Walkertown. They lasted only a few weeks, run off by a string of strange phenomena, apparently caused by the ghost of a former resident.

The Wagoners moved into the old house that summer, unpacked their belongings, and settled in. A few days later, they returned home one evening and discovered the smell of flowers in one of the bedrooms. The aroma was strong, sweet, and undeniably flowery, the smell that greets visitors to a funeral home. The following evening, another odor awoke both Mr. and Mrs. Wagoner sometime during the night. They both recognized the acrid smell of snuff in their bedroom.

Odors were one thing for the family to handle, but the next evening they were really shaken. Mr. and Mrs. Wagoner reluctantly went to bed that night, thankful that all smells in their bedroom were normal, but in the darkness, an eye appeared and watched them from the mantel near the foot of their bed. Then another eye became visible. Mr. Wagoner immediately lurched for the lights, and the couple discovered that the eyes were emanating from the two flower vases sitting apart on the corners of the mantel. They examined the vases, careful to avoid touching them, and found that the eyeballs looked real, and were staring silently out into the bedroom at the two of them. As Mrs. Wagoner nervously walked around the room, the eyes followed her from corner to corner. The eyeballs never threatened them in any way, only watched, but the Wagoners slept very little that night. The next morning the eyeballs were still watching.

That morning Mrs. Wagoner called her stepfather, trying to find some answers or encouragement for the nightmare that was getting worse. He was skeptical, to say the least, when he heard about the eyeballs in the flower vases. To prove her point, Mrs. Wagoner took the vases over to his house and showed her stepfather what had frightened her and her husband so much. He took one look at the vases and ordered her to get them out of his house. Not wanting to take the vases back with her, Mrs. Wagoner put them into her stepfather's garage. And there they sat undisturbed, until eventually the eyes disappeared.

But even with the eyeballs out of the house, mysterious events continued. In the bedroom where the smell of flowers had been detected, a light began to burn without being turned on. The first time the Wagoners noticed it, the light came on a few seconds after nearby church bells had chimed six o'clock. Then it became a regular occurrence. Every night the lights came on soon after the chimes. Certain that an intruder was responsible, the family made sure the house was locked securely, but the light continued to come on.

Mr. Wagoner, an electrician, thoroughly checked the wiring inside the lamp, and found everything to be normal. He took the bulb out of the lamp and set it on the bed, thinking he had solved the problem. A few hours later when he returned, the bulb was back in the socket and the light was on.

Wondering about their own sanity now, the couple together removed the bulb the next evening. They left the room and shut the door. Expecting something to happen-- nothing would have shocked them at this point --they stopped in the hall and waited for a few minutes outside the door. They heard a creaking noise and watched in silence as the doorknob began to slowly turn. Mr.

Wagoner reached down and opened the door, but the room was empty. The light bulb was back in the lamp and burning.

Mr. Wagoner related these events to his uncle, who scoffed and offered to sleep in the room where the light kept coming on, intending to disprove their suspicions. The light did not come on that evening, but the uncle was awakened later by a solid rapping on the window pane. Going over to the window, he saw no one, but he did notice that the screen on the outside of the window was locked securely, indicating that the knocking must have come from the inside. This was similar to what happened to the painter in the house at 909 Church Street. The uncle left immediately and refused to ever stay in the house again.

A few nights later, the family heard footsteps in the attic. Mr. Wagoner ran over to the landlady's house and borrowed a shotgun before going up to check. When he entered the dark, dusty attic, no one was there.

The Wagoners grew more frightened each day by the lack of any logical reason for what was happening. These events went on for two weeks until the family packed their things and moved out.

The family that moved in after the Wagoners also spoke of a light that came on by itself and footsteps in the attic. The landlady remembered some of the weird occurrences the Wagoners related, as well as the night Mr. Wagoner came over to borrow a gun.

The Wagoners later learned that the first event in their haunting, the smell of flowers in one of the bedrooms, had occurred on the night when Mrs. Osborne, the eighty year-old owner of the house, died. Mrs. Osborne had lived there all her life until three years earlier, when a stroke had forced her to move away. The bedroom where the scent of flowers was detected was the room where she had spent countless hours over the years playing the piano. The room where the Wagoners slept and smelled the snuff, as well as saw the eyeballs in the inanimate vases, was Mrs. Osborne's bedroom.

The landlady was her daughter.

A few years later the house was sold, and the new owners spent quite a bit on remodeling and redecorating. No more strange events occurred there. Apparently the changes were enough to convince an elderly woman that death had taken her earthly home from her.

The Ghostly Barber

MOST SUPERNATURAL STORIES involve ghosts that are seen or heard, which frighten but never harm the humans involved. But a Greensboro lady found out firsthand that nothing is worse than a malicious spirit.

A young couple, call them Roger and Mary, and their toddler daughter, Jennifer, moved from Greensboro to Columbus, Ohio almost thirty years ago. There, Roger fell in with the wrong crowd and began to dabble in black magic. His life revolved around reciting incantations and sacrificing animals. Things got worse and worse for Mary as her husband strayed farther into this dark, mysterious realm, and she feared what he might do to her or their daughter.

Mary finally packed her things, took Jennifer, and drove back to Greensboro. It was only a short time before Roger followed them. He eventually reconciled with Mary, and moved into her house, a cement block and stone bungalow. A few months later Roger suddenly died, the victim of a heart attack.

Fate had made Mary's life seem like a bad dream. Maybe now that her mysterious husband had died and the source of all her anguish was removed, she and her daughter could begin anew and create a more comfortable life. Unfortunately, Roger wasn't finished with her yet.

In the small house where they still lived, Mary and Jennifer began to be regularly disturbed by a knocking on the door, and when they would check, no one would be there. In several rooms they heard light footsteps that were barely audible. Later they heard eerie whispering. It was unnerving to be alone in a room and hear a faint voice right behind them whispering words that weren't quite distinguishable, but were very real. Visitors to the house also heard combinations of the knocking, footsteps, and whispering, and worse yet, an apparition was seen in one of the rooms. It flitted about, disappearing as quickly as it appeared, not visible long enough to be identifiable.

An even more horrible event happened. Mary awoke one morning to find a chunk of her hair had been cut off. The cut was haphazard and ragged, as a child might have done with a razor. When it happened again a few weeks later, both Mary and Jennifer felt that Roger was somehow responsible. He was probably still vindictive over something that had happened in his life, perhaps Mary's leaving him. They wondered if this was another curse from his experience in black magic.

The nighttime haircuts continued. Mary and Jennifer dreaded the arrival of each night, frightened of what they might find in the morning. Mary got rid of all the scissors and razors in the house, but that didn't help. Jennifer sometimes wondered if she were being possessed at night by her dead father and clipping her mother's hair without either of them knowing it. Mary locked her bedroom door several times, only to find the next morning that her hair was ruined with a new cut. Occasionally, parts of her head were shaved. Mary even nailed the bedroom door shut, to no avail. The torture of the haircuts still went on, but at least the mother and daughter knew that they were not responsible. Each time this happened, both felt they had spent the night more in a trance than asleep, and this was the only way Mary could explain how she was able to sleep through the countless times her hair was butchered.

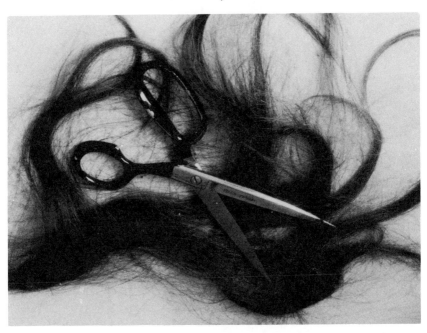

Somehow Mary and Jennifer lived like this for twenty years until they contacted a parapsychologist, who told them the hostile ghost of Roger was indeed living in the house. The parapsychologist worked to drive Roger out. The nightly haircuts stopped.

When this story was first recorded four years ago in *The Ghostly Register* by Arthur Myers, the mother and daughter asked that their real names and address not be used, and their wishes have been respected. Their story shows that it's wise to patch up human differences before reaching the grave.

The Slave Who Came with the House

MR. AND MRS. J.D. SWAIM discovered an extra occupant in their house near Pfafftown, who apparently came with the house. Although uninvited, this occupant was definitely there first.

Mrs. Swaim was watching television alone late one summer night not too long after she and her husband had moved into their new residence. The large house was situated right beside an old graveyard for slaves who died in the nineteenth century. The room was dark except for the flickering black and white images coming from the small television screen. Mrs. Swaim noticed that something in the room changed just before she felt her right shoulder go cold, as if it had been stuck into a freezer. She sat very still, frightened by what was happening to her, and thought of calling for her husband who was asleep. Her shoulder ached from the chill. Mrs. Swaim opened her mouth to yell for her husband, but she changed her mind for some reason, and said, "Stop it, Charlie!" For a second she was puzzled by her strange words; she knew no Charlie. However, her shoulder instantly came back to life and she felt as if things were as they had been before.

Mrs. Swaim discussed the strange occurrence with her husband, and they both dismissed it as her imagination;

however, it wasn't long before more mysterious things happened. One evening Mrs. Swaim heard the front door open and someone enter. She went to meet the visitor, sure it was their neighbor, but when she reached the door it was closed tightly and locked. No one had entered.

One dark night sometime later both Mr. and Mrs. Swaim heard a noise in their closet just after they had gone to bed. Since they were both sleepy and a little apprehensive, they ignored the noise, which sounded like metal rubbing against metal. The next morning when they checked the closet, their clothes were fine, but all of the empty clothes hangers were scattered on the floor in disarray, as if they had been carelessly knocked off the rack.

By this time, the Swaims accepted the fact that their house was occupied by a spirit. The ghost they called Charlie was mischievous but not harmful, so they never felt threatened by it, and eventually Charlie became almost part of the family. He let himself be heard many times. Once Mrs. Swaim heard Mr. Swaim upstairs cleaning his office, but when she checked, her husband was in the bedroom, sound asleep. Charlie had been doing some ghostly cleaning.

One night the Swaims arrived home late and hurried to get to bed since they had to be up early the next morning. They saw a clear imprint of someone's head in the pillow on Mrs. Swaim's side of the bed. The imprint had not been there when they left, and they were sure that no one had been in the house while they were gone. Apparently, Charlie had left a photograph of himself in the only way he could.

Charlie remained mischievous. A neighbor's daughter was playing in an upstairs room of the Swaim house, while the adults talked downstairs. The child was loud and got into everything she could reach. Meanwhile, her father was scoffing at the Swaims' tales about Charlie. A few minutes later the child decided to come downstairs, but couldn't get the door to the room open. She screamed loudly, summoning the adults, who tugged and shoved and heaved, but the door was stuck.

On a whim, Mrs. Swaim said once more, "Stop it, Charlie." The next pull opened the door easily.

The girl's father looked at the Swaims and said, "I suppose you're going to tell me that was Charlie holding the door." The door proceeded to close right in front of them.

Mr. Swaim said, "Yeah, it's Charlie. If you don't believe it, tell me what *you* think it is." The door opened again by itself. The neighbor left, convinced.

Charlie found another way to communicate a few years later. The Swaims took a picture of their granddaughter standing in the backyard. When the picture was developed, behind the girl stood the fuzzy outline of a man. It was the image of an elderly, black man, holding a baby goat. The Swaims decided that Charlie must have been one of the slaves who had died and been buried in the nearby graveyard. There had been goats raised on the surrounding land near the house.

The picture is now in the possession of the granddaughter, who lives in another part of the country.

Why did Charlie live in the house? What had occurred during his life or at his death to cause his spirit to remain in this world? The Swaims were unable to find the answers to these questions. Charlie's mystery will probably remain unsolved forever.

Charlie grew closer to the family as each year went by. After her husband passed away, Mrs. Swaim lived alone in her home, except that the friendly spirit was there to keep her company. She is currently planning to sell the house and is upset about leaving Charlie, but she's sure it won't take him long to introduce and endear himself to the next occupants.

Robah's Revenge

DELA MASON (not her real name) used to go to Salem Cemetery with her friends and party. Like most teenagers, they were out to have a good time, felt immortal themselves, and didn't have much respect for the dead.

They strolled through the graveyard during weekend nights, when there wasn't anything else to do, for the spooky thrill of it. Dela, now in her thirties, says that she didn't really believe in ghosts until something happened after one of these graveyard jaunts when she was sixteen.

She and her roving group of friends were walking around the old mausoleums and tombstones after dark with a flashlight and a bottle of wine. They came upon the grave of Robah Gray, and they sat down for a rest. Her boyfriend, Ted, shined the light on the headstone in front of them.

"Mind if we sit with you, Robah?" he asked. Soon the rest of the group began to joke with the departed Robah: "Wanna swig of wine, Robah? Did you have a gal, Robah? Don't you get sick of being stuck in the graveyard, Robah?" --that sort of thing.

They polished off the bottle and climbed into Dela's Volkswagen Bug, beckoning Robah to join them.

Dela drove home, after dropping off her boyfriend and the other couple. When she got home, her parents were already asleep so she made herself a sandwich and sat in front of the TV.

The TV switched off as she was watching it, but she didn't think anything of it, because the set was plugged into a multi-socket adapter with many other cords, and she figured that there was a short in there somewhere. She got up and jiggled the cords, trying to get the TV back on. It didn't work, so she turned off the set and went to bed, thinking the thing was just on the blink.

Just as she was falling asleep, she heard the TV come on full blast. She ran into the den and turned it off, fearing that it would wake up her parents. She stood there scratching her head, and trying to figure out how the set had come on.

"Dela, what on earth are you doing, turning the TV up so loud?" her mother called from the top of the stairs.

"It came on by itself," she replied. "I was in bed."

"Did you leave it on?" her yawning mother asked, walking down to the stair landing.

"No. It wasn't even working. I fooled with the plug, gave up, and turned the thing off."

"Well, you probably just think you did," her mother said as she returned to bed.

The next day Dela was alone in the house, eating a snack and watching TV, when the phone rang. She set her snack, a bowl of potato chips and a glass of soda, on the TV and answered the phone in the kitchen. It was Ted. As they were talking she heard her glass crash to the floor.

"I'll call you back, Ted. My drink just spilled."

She hung up and walked back into the den to find the first indication that something was awry. The glass hadn't just spilled. It looked as if it had been hurled across the room against the opposite wall, along with the bowl of potato chips. The soda was dripping down the wall toward the scattering of glass and chips below.

Dela's first reaction was that somebody else was in the house, and she had to get out. She ran to the front door, turned

the knob, and opened it. Then, feeling she was at a safe place, she stopped and yelled, "Is anyone home? Mom?"

Silence.

Dela shut the door and sat on the front stoop, until her mother returned from shopping. She told her mother what had happened and they walked into the house together and surveyed the mess.

Dela was very cautious, refusing to even walk near it. They checked out every room and found nobody.

"Do you think this house is haunted?" Dela asked suddenly.

"Of course not. It's not even five years old."

"Well, maybe it was built on top of a graveyard."

Her mother just shook her head quietly and gazed at her.

Odd things continued to happen, but they only seemed to happen to Dela and only in the den. Once she was listening to an eight-track tape of Led Zeppelin and she heard a voice mumbling over the music. When the same song came on again, the voice was gone.

Another time she was in the den, reading, and her father was upstairs. She left her book on the sofa, upside-down and open to mark her page. She walked from the kitchen to the backyard to check on a shirt that was drying on the line. When she returned to the den, she found the book on the other side of the room, on the floor in front of the fireplace. Of all the family pictures on the mantel, the one of her taken as an adolescent was lying beside the book, the glass shattered. Dela went and got her father who said he had heard nothing.

Dela no longer spent any time in the den. She begged her parents to move out of the house, and they were becoming worried about Dela's mental health.

Until this time, she had discussed these experiences with only her parents, but she felt that they were turning their backs on her. She began spending every night she could away from home.

One night when she was out with Ted, she broke down

and told him about what had happened to her.

"Well, it must have been Robah," he said without hesitation, as if it were the most logical thing in the world. "Remember you asked him to come along with us that night. He probably jumped in the Bug and came home with you."

"I don't know," she said. "You think so?"

"Sure," he said, dragging on his cigarette. "We'll just have to take him back to the grave."

So the next night while her parents were eating dinner out, they went to the house and into the den and began calling to Robah. "Come on, Robah, out to the car."

Several times they walked to the car and back to the den, in case Robah got confused about where he was going. Then they drove back to Salem Cemetery.

They pulled up beside the grave and opened the door. "Okay, Robah. Out you go. Come on, You're home."

They lingered around the grave for a while, then Ted said, "Let's split!" and both he and Dela quickly raced back to the car and drove off.

The disturbances in Dela's den ceased, and she never went fooling around in graveyards again.

The Rabid Ghost

IT IS BELIEVED that if a person is mentally disturbed at the moment of death, his soul isn't able to attain peace, and is trapped between two worlds in a frantic state. It fights and knocks about, seemingly unaware of life around it. This was the case with the death of Tommy Leonard. Leonard (not his real name) came upon hard times. An alcoholic, he had a hard time holding down a job, and through his drunken haze, he watched as his wife moved out. His children had gone their own ways years before. Thus, he was left with nothing but an empty house and a dozen hunting dogs. He had always been close to his animals. Perhaps because of his loneliness, he became even more attached to his dogs, allowing them free rein in the house. He stopped leaving the house. He had a still, and the liquor it produced became his only solace. There was nobody around to be concerned about his welfare. His days were spent numbing himself to the point of unconsciousness.

Then both his decaying mental and physical health took a turn for the worse. One night one of his beloved dogs turned on him and attacked him. Although he survived the attack, the damage had already been done, for the dogs had contracted rabies, and he, either being unaware of their state or unable to comprehend the seriousness of the situation, did not seek help for the dogs or for himself.

The delusions that Tommy Leonard experienced were probably horrifying. It is known that rabies produces extreme dementia in its victims, animal and human. Its symptoms include hallucinations, combativeness, confusion, and aberrations of thought, along with the grave physical symptoms: vomiting, muscle spasms, and seizures that eventually lead to coma and death. Even with treatment, the prognosis of a rabies victim is grim, and Leonard had no treatment whatsoever.

His condition certainly followed the usual course: episodes of mental derangement followed by periods of lucidness, during which the disease progressed. It was probably during these periods that Leonard reached for the bottle. This could have gone on for days or weeks, nobody can be sure. He never had a chance.

At some point, Leonard found it necessary to squeeze himself under the box springs of his metal frame bed, a mere eight inches off the floor. This was in the bedroom on the first floor of the house. There he died, probably spending his last hours in terror and confusion, hiding perhaps from his dogs, perhaps from something that didn't exist at all.

His decomposed body was discovered a week later by a neighbor. His house was a shambles, and the dogs that still lived were pacing the place, trying to get out.

Six years later, long after the dogs were removed and destroyed, the house he had occupied in Walnut Cove was cleaned up and sold to Mr. and Mrs. Davidson, a middle-aged couple who planned to retire there. They knew that Mr. Leonard had died there, but were not spooked in the least. They were not easily given to believing in ghosts. They were surprised to find that the place did not bring them the peace they sought.

They lived there a few weeks, hearing noises occasionally, but attributing them to the settling of the foundation of the old house.

Later, they realized that the noises were something more.

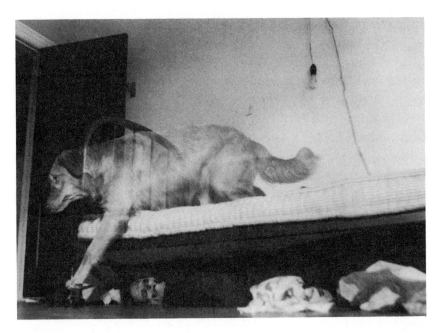

They sat in the living room one evening, watching TV, when suddenly there was a loud clanking in their bedroom, which sounded curiously as if someone were beating against something metal and hollow. Although it originated in the bedroom, the noise echoed throughout the whole house. The Davidsons sat frozen for a while.

"It's probably some animal that got in there through the hole in the window screen," Mr. Davidson assured his wife. He got up, took a broom out of the closet, and padded into the bedroom. He checked the closet, behind the dressers and under the bed. Scratching his head, he came back out of the bedroom. His wife waited outside the door.

"Whatever it was, it's gone now," he said. "I guess it found its way out."

They settled back down in front of the TV. Suddenly the same noise shook the house again, but this time it was more frantic. It was louder, growing into a cacophony of groans, howls, bangs, and bed squeaks. It ceased all of a sudden, leaving the house quiet except for the TV which continued to play.

Mr. Davidson was much more cautious about entering the room this time. He slowly opened the door, as his wife stood behind him, wringing her hands. Again, he looked around the room, and found nothing. When he came back out to the hall, the door suddenly slammed behind him under its own volition.

Nothing out of the ordinary happened for the rest of the night. Shaken, the Davidsons decided to sleep in the living room. These noises continued for several months, often the strange howl accompanied them. Sometimes it was just the banging on metal, short and loud. Sometimes it was a long, drawn-out groan. The Davidsons eventually got used to their ghost.

They often heard it when they were sitting on the porch or in the living room, but never when they were in the bedroom. It ceased altogether when the weather became colder, and the Davidsons thought they were free of the ghost. But it came back in the spring. It seemed to prefer spring and summer to cool weather for its activity.

Once when Mrs. Davidson tried to get into the bedroom she found that the door had become latched from the inside, something that would have been impossible unless someone had been in the room.

The ghost seemed to want to get attention, but didn't make noise when someone was in the room with it. Perhaps owing to its loneliness in life, it was satisfied having someone nearby. When the Davidsons were sleeping in there, it was inactive, however, if the room was empty, it carried on until somone entered. They heard it most often when they were sitting out on the front porch.

The Davidsons decided to tough it out. They weren't about to let this frustrated spirit chase them away. They did some research and found out about Tommy Leonard's demise, in the very room where they slept, in the summer.

They still live in the house, and have come to tolerate the clanking and squeaking of the bed springs, having a certain amount of sympathy for the ghost of a man who died an unsettling, lonely death.

Satan's Strongholds

There are some areas that have more paranormal activity than others. For whatever reason, these areas are frequented by haunts that torment the humans who happen to be there at the wrong time. Two of these strongholds are located in the Triad.

The Taz Place: Land of the Dead

TAZ PILLMAN WORKED tirelessly as a slave on his master's plantation, always believing that a better life must be just around the corner. Born in captivity, he grew to be a tall, wiry young man, deceptively strong. After living through the horror that engulfed the nation called the Civil War, he was flooded with the euphoria of freedom, having been granted eighty-five acres of rich, wooded land in southern Surry County. Taking his sweetheart, Leila, to be his wife, Taz built a small log cabin in the center of his land, and set about turning the woodlands into farmland. The area, which bordered the Fisher River, consisted of rolling hills and a lake fed by a cold, clean spring. The Pillmans believed that they had found their paradise, but less than a year after their marriage, Taz began to get an unsettling, eerie feeling at times. He believed that this strange sensation originated from somewhere on his land. Legends abounded about the area since it was an ancient Cherokee Indian burial ground, and indeed a hidden cave containing mounds of human bones was discovered near the river. Also, armies from at least two wars had passed over the land. Exactly what it was he felt, Taz had no idea.

The bliss returned for a short time when Leila gave birth to a beautiful set of twin boys, and the joy of newborn babies filled the cabin, but this lasted only a few days. One night the twins mysteriously became ill and died. Heartbroken, Taz put the tiny bodies on a shelf to cool, in preparation for their burial the next morning, as was the custom of the day.

Unable to sleep, Taz sat alone and stared at the steadily dying fire burning in the hearth. The hours passed by slowly that night as Taz silently grieved, but sometime after midnight, he was drawn back to his senses by the sound of a faint knock on the door. At first, Taz was uncertain whether he had actually heard anything, but once again, he heard the faint tapping of knuckles on wood. That cold, eerie feeling filled the room, stronger than ever, and he considered not answering. However, common sense told Taz that it could only be one of his neighbors, there to console him at that late hour. So he walked over and opened the door. There he found a man, dressed very neatly in a fine white shirt with splendid lace around the buttons and cuffs, dark wool pants, and leather boots, obviously a gentleman, but the man had no head! His neck still displayed a jagged edge where he had been decapitated, and blood bubbled up out of the neck, spurting like a fountain each time the man's heart beat. The blood ran down the white shirt, turning it instantly to a violent red. A neighbor perhaps, but not of this world.

Taz staggered back from the hideous sight as he tried to yell, tried to run, tried to defend himself, tried to do anything, but the shock and terror overwhelmed him. He sank to the floor, unconscious.

When Taz opened his eyes, the fresh light of morning cast a glow through the room. His wife stood over him and scolded him for having slept on the floor, and for having left the door open all night. When Taz told her what he had seen the night before, she tried to comfort him, telling him that it had to have been his grief that made him imagine seeing the headless man. Taz was wondering if he had only experienced a horrible nightmare, until he looked at the shelf where he had set the bodies of the twins, and found it was empty. The bodies were

The Taz Place

gone. A search was conducted throughout the county but no sign of the dead infants was ever found. Had the headless man taken the infants in revenge for some inhuman act that had taken his own life?

Taz lived there for the rest of his life, and fortunately never had anything quite so frightening happen to him again, but he did hear strange noises, such as the sounds of a mysterious horse that was never seen. He continued to sense that eerie feeling from time to time. Having seen the headless man, he had a renewed respect for the world of the dead.

He also caught glimpses of a large cat, possibly a panther, that vanished into nowhere. Taz called it the "Devil Cat."

After Taz Pillman's death near the turn of the century, the land was passed to his heirs and eventually sold to the Poindexter family, but the legends surrounding the strange phenomenon there continued. About sixty years ago a boy named William, who lived near the land still called the Taz Place, learned firsthand about the legend. One fine summer

Saturday he helped the Poindexters in the fields until sundown, then stayed late into the night, playing and talking, since he would be able to sleep late the next day. William finally began the long walk home along the lonely dirt road through the darkest night he would ever know.

Although it was almost midnight, William knew the road well and made good time through the darkness. A noise caught his attention, and he quickly recognized it as a conversation between two neighbor girls, talking about how they could avoid getting into trouble for coming home so late from a community dance. As they came up the road behind him, William was glad for the company of the young ladies on that night, but a sixteen year-old boy couldn't pass up the thrill of scaring the girls as they came by. So William hid in the woods beside a huge oak tree and waited for his chance.

Listening carefully as the voices came closer, William stood perfectly still and planned his devilry, trying not to laugh out loud. Suddenly an odd noise from right behind him made William whirl around. His eyes were well adjusted to the darkness, and he saw something that made his breath stop. There stood a ghostly, white horse only inches away, its eyes two slits of darkness, cold and unfeeling. It got worse as William looked up, for sitting on the horse was a finely dressed rider, splendidly made up for a ride, except that he had no head. Blood gushed out of his neck and cascaded over a white shirt. William nearly died right there.

At some point in the past, someone who claimed to know had told William that if a live human being ran from a ghost, that person would die. So William turned around and walked away. His mind was so terrified that it shut down, only compelling him to walk as fast as he could!

Several minutes later, William's parents, who were sleeping in their bed, were awakened by the sound of pounding feet coming down the road toward their house. They rushed downstairs, just in time to see the door crash open, ripping right off the hinges, and William collapse on the floor in front of them. When he finally regained consciousness an hour later, he was still shaking and remembered the horse and ghastly rider, but the journey home, including walking right through the door, was a complete blank. He later found out the girls he had planned to scare made it home without incident, never knowing what had saved them from a boy's prank.

The horse and rider were never seen again, but there were several nights when the sounds of a horse were heard at more than one house. Each time there was no visitor, and the next morning there were no tracks to be found. Could this have been the ghostly pair prowling, possibly looking for the lost head?

About forty-five years ago, Ed, a relative of the Poindexters who lived in a house near the Taz Place, had the cruel fate to lose his wife prematurely. Their plans and dreams of growing old together were dashed by her death. The man continued on with his life, working as much as possible to avoid having time to mourn his loss.

One evening after a hard day's labor, Ed was driving home in a wagon drawn by an old workhorse. As they passed an empty field next to the Taz Place, only a few hundred yards from his home, the nag suddenly stopped and snorted. Looking over at the field, he saw a woman picking flowers. Something about the woman seemed familiar and he stood up in the wagon to see better. His blood ran cold when the woman turned to face him. It was his wife, wearing the same dress she had been buried in! Her attractive face looked just as he remembered.

Ed was stunned and a little frightened as he tried to believe what he saw in the field, but the horse suddenly bolted forward, slinging him out of the wagon and down to the ground. He was bruised but ignored the pain and ran toward his wife, only he found that the field was completely empty. She had vanished.

Thinking that his relatives probably would not believe

him, Ed kept the incident to himself for years. When he finally broke down and told the story, he was startled to find that the other family members had no doubt of what he had seen, due to their own unique experiences around the Taz Place.

The last strange thing to happen around there was several years ago when the "Devil Cat" reappeared and attacked a teenaged neighbor, who was riding a horse home from a party at the old Taz house. As she rode down the same road that William had stumbled along that night years before, a huge cat leaped down from the limb of a tree onto the rump of her horse. She was able to see that the cat was blacker than the darkest night, with fierce red eyes that glared at her with apparent hatred. The horse was terrified and bolted away, nearly throwing her off in the process. The cat was thrown to the ground, but instantly turned and chased them, while the girl hung on for her life. The cat was incredibly fast and caught them again, raking its claws over the horse. Blood spurted all over the girl. It was only a matter of time before the cat's claws would find her skin. She thought quickly and yanked off her blouse, throwing it to the ground beside the big cat, who stopped for a second to investigate. The chase resumed and the cat caught them again a short distance down the road, but she threw off a shoe and gained a few more seconds and a few more precious yards toward her home.

Her family was waiting in the house for her return. The door burst open and she ran inside, crying hysterically, completely naked, and covered with blood. Her mother screamed, then rushed to her aid. The girl was unharmed, the blood on her being the horse's. Her family tried to comfort her and listened as she told her strange story, that ended with her jumping off the horse in the yard and running for the door, with the cat tearing up the drive toward the house. Some of her bloodstained clothes were later recovered but the horse was never found.

Today the Taz Place is still in the Poindexter family and is still the subject of endless lore. There have been reports of a huge cat spotted around the area. The cave containing the mounds of Indian bones can still be reached with a considerable and dangerous hike, but the family has always respected the burial grounds and never allowed artifacts to be removed. There is a pool, fed by a spring, that many say has no bottom. Several times over the years, rocks were tied to long ropes and lowered into the pool. The rocks never struck anything solid. No one lives on the land, which is used now only for recreation, but the legends are alive and will be forever.

Many thanks go to Phyllis Townsend for listening carefully to her grandparents, parents, aunts, uncles, and cousins when they discussed the "haints" that became a part of the Poindexters' lives, and for her efforts to let us record these stories, which included a guided tour of the area.

The Evans Place: Where Evil Spirits Reign

THERE ARE PEOPLE in this world who, for whatever reason, are more sensitive to paranormal activity than others. Cora Pearson, a native of Forsyth County, is endowed with this gift. To this day, Cora's dreams foreshadow the future. They have predicted many of the most tragic experiences in her life, the most salient of which was her father's death. Not only did she dream that he would have a heart attack, but she knew the exact time. The next day she warned family members who were shocked when it came to pass just as she had dreamed it.

Cora has always felt a little intimidated by her abilities and has sought out parapsychologists in an effort to better understand her own gift. (Cora is now an upstanding member of the community and asked that her real name not be used, however, others have corroborated her claim of extra-sensory perception.)

Of course, some psychic people live in an area of low paranormal activity and thus, never fully realize their potential, but Cora didn't have this problem. When she was still a small child, her family moved to an area of Forsyth County, which, according to Cora, was mired in supernatural forces. Cora sensed that the house her family lived in was central to this activity, and also that mostly evil spirits had a stronghold there.

Their house was located on the left side of the street, just after the first curve on Evans Road.

The road was named for the Evans family, a wealthy family who owned a large farm on it. Cora Pearson was the daughter of sharecroppers who worked the Evans' land. The Pearsons moved into the house when Cora was just a toddler.

It was rumored that one of the Evans men had murdered someone in the living room of the Pearsons' house, and that because of his power and affluence, he was never indicted. If a murder and cover-up did occur, the victim certainly must have been from outside the community and of no consequence to the neighbors. Still, the rumor persisted among neighbors and in the Pearson household.

When the Pearsons moved into the house in the early nineteen-thirties, there was what appeared to be a large blood stain on the wooden floor in the living room. The stain was dark and ominous, and Cora's father immediately set about removing it from the floor. He first tried planing the wood, and the stain was sanded away, but within days it resurfaced. Then Mr. Pearson decided to cover the stain with linoleum, but gradually over the next week, the stain came through the linoleum, starting out yellow and eventually turning dark brown. Mr. Pearson then covered that piece of linoleum with yet another piece, but the stain could not be stopped. They had no choice but to accept it.

They also heard knocks and bumps emanating from the living room at all hours of the day and night. Often the noises would awaken the whole family.

On several occasions, Mrs. Pearson saw wispy, illuminated objects floating close to the ceiling. Since she could find no logical explanation for this, she told nobody about it until recently. At the time there was enough talk about the haunts, and she didn't want to rile anyone up even more.

Soon after the Pearsons arrived, they heard the neighbors talk of yet another nearby murder that took place a few years before they moved in. A husband had shot and killed his wife

Barn where hanging took place

in a house further down the road from the Pearsons' house. Apparently everyone around had been shocked that such a nice man would commit such a heinous crime.

When Cora was still a child, the cryptic mystery of the area was augmented when the husband of Mrs. Pearson's best friend and neighbor was found hanging in a nearby barn. Although the death was ruled as a suicide, none of the neighbors believed it. As far as they were concerned, the man had no reason for taking his own life. He had a loving family and financial security. Some suspected that local men had hanged him out of jealousy.

There were those who felt that something evil and mysterious had taken root and was turning a portion of the local menfolk into monsters. Cora could sense it happening to her own father who began to rule his family with an iron fist, beating his wife and children into submission.

Not long after the supposed suicide, a neighbor's baby died suddenly and mysteriously, shocking the neighbors even more.

And then there were the apparitions around the Pearson household. Few people cared to visit the Pearsons after dark, including Tom and Ossie Smith, a couple who lived at the end of Evans Road. Like the Pearsons, they suspected that the area was cloaked in evil, having witnessed things floating around the outside of the house at night.

One day Cora's little sister, Rita, was playing with her dolls in the attic when she dashed out of the house, white and shaken. Mrs. Pearson tried to calm the girl, but the child was in a frantic state.

Refusing to return to the house, the girl swore that she had seen three ghosts of different sizes floating together near the ceiling of the attic. All of the apparitions had fixed eyes that gazed straight ahead, seemingly oblivious to her. They moved together as if they were clouds being propelled by a gentle, steady breeze. When they came to the wall, they passed through it effortlessly. Although they were distinctly human, Rita couldn't determine whether they were male or female.

Cora's grandmother, a very religious woman, also saw the ghost of an elderly woman with long, flowing white hair hovering outside the attic, gazing through a lower window at Cora as she slept. Often when the grandmother saw this, she felt something hit her foot which she described as feeling like a "bolt of lightning". This happened on more than one occasion, and soon the grandmother, like the Smiths, refused to come over anymore at night. Cora felt that this ghost was acting as her guardian angel, protecting her from the evil inherent in the place.

One time, Cora, Rita, their brother and cousin were all playing in the loft of a barn, in the woods not far from their house, when suddenly a terrifying creature appeared before them. It was a large bear with red eyes, matted fur, and slobber drooling off of its red tongue. It spoke in a deep, evil voice, beckoning them to come down from the loft into its clutches. Cora felt very mesmerized and drawn to the creature, but she mustered all of her power to turn and run away, finding out afterwards that all the other children had already hightailed it out the loft window and down the ladder. Apparently the other children didn't feel as attracted to the creature as Cora.

These children, now adults, all remember encountering this creature in the loft. It is a secret they have kept until this time, knowing that the world would never believe them.

Today Cora is sure that it was Satan.

A man who today lives in the house next to the barn where the hanging occurred says that nothing out of the ordinary has ever happened to him. Perhaps it has something to do with the Pearson house having been torn down -- there is nothing left there now but an old outhouse, slumped toward the ground. Or maybe it is because nobody around is psychic enough to pick up on it.

Ghosts, Inc.

In the present day hustle-bustle world with no time for interruptions, what would happen if a ghost wandered into a business? Here are the stories of two that did just that.

The Furniture Phantom

THE SAN-MOR FURNITURE COMPANY moved into a building on Peace Street in Thomasville in 1973. One evening a few days later, in the main workroom, owner Victor Couch spotted a dim form that walked by and disappeared. As the weeks went by and Mr. Couch saw the shadowy figure more and more, he questioned his own vision and wondered if he had lost a marble somewhere along the way.

So Mr. Couch visited a psychiatrist and spent a half-hour talking about his problems. When his time was up, the psychiatrist asked him the real reason for the visit, and Mr. Couch reluctantly admitted to having seen an apparition in the factory. The psychiatrist responded, "Why the hell didn't you tell me that in the first place?" Mr. Couch left with a lighter wallet, but feeling comforted that what he was seeing was not a figment of his imagination.

Other workers in the factory spotted the ghost and began to call him Lucifer. Later, one of the workers called him Lucas, and the name stuck. (The ghost in Dana Auditorium is also called Lucas, apparently a popular name for wandering spirits.) Several times employees heard stacks of lumber falling, but found nothing out of order when they investigated. One night just before locking up, Mr. Couch spread out tools in a certain order on a table. When he opened the factory the next morning, he found that Lucas, not to be outdone, had gathered the tools together into a pile.

Lucas appears to be a middle-aged man, about 5 feet 10 inches tall, with hair that is visible, but too dim to tell the color. He appears as a hazy figure, more transparent than opaque. His facial features are not discernible, nor are his hands and feet, but his clothes are very distinctive. Lucas wears a long-sleeved, checked shirt, and khaki work pants.

He normally comes out after 3:30 p.m. and loves the nighttime, however Mr. Couch's daughter spotted Lucas disappearing behind some boxes around 9:00 a.m. one morning. The ghost has been spotted hundreds of times by dozens of people, and has become one of the most documented ghosts on record, having been investigated by TV, radio, newspapers, and well-known parapsychologists. One psychic researcher reported that Lucas grabbed her shoulder during a seance. A camera crew from the television show, *That's Incredible*, spent three nights in the factory several years ago. They brought expensive camera equipment and planned to film and photograph Lucas. Sure enough, they spotted him and aimed their cameras in his direction, but when the film was developed, it showed no sign of Lucas.

However, Lucas has been spotted on film twice. Three ladies had a photograph taken of themselves one evening inside the factory, and the picture showed a blurry figure that was barely visible to their right. Also, a local TV station came to film Lucas, but as he was shy that evening, they thought they were out of luck. Just to have something to do, one of the cameramen shot footage of Mr. Couch walking down a short stairway, and when the film was developed, an indistinct, milky outline appeared to be moving just behind Mr. Couch. Lucas is sensitive about whom he will be photographed with.

Lucas' origin is mysterious, but it is believed to be from about sixty-five years ago when there was a barn on the lot. A man was hanged from one of the rafters of the barn, a victim either of suicide or foul play. When Mr. Couch and a

Former San-Mor factory

parapsychologist were going through the building, they came to a spot where they felt a cold sensation that made the hair on the back of their necks stand on end. They decided that must be the spot where the hanging took place.

Lucas has never frightened Mr. Couch, but he has rattled a few nerves over the years, like when he forced the night shift at San-Mor to be cancelled. The workers spent so much time each night looking out for Lucas that production fell drastically.

Mr. Couch's brother, who lived beside the factory, was walking his dog one evening, when the dog suddenly stiffened and looked anxiously at something that was not visible to his master. The dog yelped and took off in a mad dash toward home. Mr. Couch describes his brother as a large man, but the terrified dog was more powerful, because his brother was unable to hold onto the leash.

One night around 11:00 p.m., Mr. Couch and five other men encountered Lucas. One man was bending over a box, ready to lift it, when he spotted a pair of legs behind him and asked whoever it was to help him lift the box. When he turned and saw the legs belonged to Lucas, and the other men were standing several feet away, watching the whole scene with wide eyes, he said only, "Uh-oh," before launching himself toward the exit. Mr. Couch reported the five workers left like they'd been shot out of a gun, not bothering to punch the time clock.

Late another night, two policemen were making their rounds through the city when they pulled their car behind the factory and spotted a figure. With their lights shining on the man, they went to investigate, whereupon the figure disappeared, walking right through the wall into the factory.

Mr. Couch says that he has been contacted by people from all over the world who have heard about Lucas. One lady from England told him her factory was home for a while to a ghost, who actually seemed to be helping with some of the work. One day several of the other workers gathered around the ghost and began asking it questions about the spirit world and why it had chosen to remain in this one. The spirit promptly vanished and was never seen again. The woman said she wished the ghost had stayed and the workers vanished, since the ghost worked harder.

Although Lucas never really worked, Mr. Couch thinks Lucas may have earned his keep. More than once, Couch has found windows in the factory that were pried open during the night, probably by burglars, but each time it was evident the intruder had stopped before entering the window. If the first thing they saw upon looking inside the factory was Lucas, that would be a powerful crime deterrent.

Mr. Couch has retired now and San-Mor no longer operates in the building, but Lucas is still there, showing himself when he feels like it, and keeping the secrets of the dead.

The Spirit that Ran the Radio Station

OBSESSION is a common cause of spirits remaining in this world. Even a popular radio station like WBIG in Greensboro was not immune to habitation by an obsessive spirit.

Major Edney Ridge, a former cavalry officer and U.S. Marshall, managed the station from 1929 until his death in 1949, and apparently continued to manage from the basement until WBIG ceased broadcasting in 1987. During his life, Major Ridge was completely devoted to keeping the functions of the station running smoothly, and consistently worked ten to twelve hour days.

Employees of the station who worked the night shift often heard someone climbing up and down the stairs to the basement. Visitors to the basement during the day--there weren't many during the evening, understandably--regularly heard bumps and knocking, and saw things fall over for no reason.

A local psychic investigated the WBIG basement and reported that she sensed the ghost of Major Ridge had been unable to leave his beloved station. He stayed downstairs near an old style turntable, the type he knew well.

The psychic reported that the major was harmless and relatively happy, but frustrated that he could not communicate

71

as he wished. When asked what the major was doing down in the basement, she replied, "Running the station."

He apparently looked much as he did when alive; gray hair, bulge around the middle, wearing a tweed jacket, and smoking a huge cigar. His one flaw was that his socks didn't match, but that probably doesn't mean much to a ghost.

The major was popular during his life, and was vital to the growth and long life of the AM station. Even after his death, the major remained popular, as the employees of WBIG voted to let his ghost remain in the basement. Some of the female employees of the station said they felt safer with Major Ridge there. If there was trouble, they knew the major would rush to protect them, just as he would have when he was alive.

All that's left now is a road bearing the name of Edney Ridge. When the station ended its operations and the building was torn down in 1987, it was time at last for the major to retire and leave radio to the young, or at least to the living.

Well-Known Triad Hauntings

Here are three Triad ghost stories that are familiar not only to local residents, but also to readers around the world.

Little Red Man--Apparently Still Inactive

NO BOOK on Triad ghosts would be complete without an account of the Little Red Man, the spritely Moravian ghost who made his presence known in the Single Brothers House in Old Salem. His story has been thoroughly described in *An Illustrated Guide to Ghosts and Mysterious Occurrences in the Old North State* by Nancy Roberts, and *Tarheel Ghosts* by John Harden.

For those who may not have already heard of him, here is his story:

In 1766, Andreas Kremser came to Bethabara from Pennsylvania with a group of Moravian settlers. He moved from there to Salem in 1772. Perhaps because of his small stature, he was assigned the job of chimney sweep. He is known to have been a rather high-spirited man, because when an outbreak of measles was blamed on insufficiently cleaned chimneys, he not only criticized the construction of the chimneys, but also the amount of work laid on his shoulders alone. This was atypical of the Moravians whose culture expected them to sacrifice for the good of the community.

Kremser's job later changed. First he became a cook and then a shoemaker. Like most other unmarried Moravian men, he lived in the Single Brothers House in Salem. The men in the house learned different trades and performed many services for the community.

One night after a church service, Kremser went down with some other men to excavate the deep cellar to make room for an addition to the building. They did this by digging out the lower end of the earthen wall and allowing the overhang to fall. Apparently this was a method often used to extend cellars.

The young men were motivated to begin this work after eleven at night, which indicates the kind of devotion these folks had to seeing a job done. Perhaps they had already put in a full day and were forced to put the excavation off until this late hour. One can only imagine how dark and dirty the work must have been, and how easily fatigued the young men became doing it.

As Andreas and the others were busy digging out the wall, one of the brothers saw that the earth above the workers was loosening. He shouted for them to move back to safety. All of them were able to jump out of the way in time except Andreas, who was on his knees. The ledge of earth fell on top of him, pinning him underneath.

The others worked furiously, digging the soil off of him until they saw his red jacket. They pulled him free and saw that he had a mangled leg. It is almost certain that he had internal injuries as well, for he was in a great deal of pain. The doctor came and tried to let blood from his arm, but Andreas was already dying, and little blood would come.

The Moravian records report his time of departure as two a.m., March 26, 1786. Andreas was thirty-three at the time of his death.

Not long after his death he was spotted by some of the brothers who first heard him tapping just like he had done during his life as a shoemaker. They also occasionally saw him float down the hallway, a small apparition clothed in a red jacket. All the men and boys were aware that he lived among them, and every unknown sound in the building was attributed to him.

When the Single Brothers House was converted to a widow's home, the Little Red Man continued to make his

Single Brothers House

presence known, once motioning with his finger to a little deaf girl to come play with him, another time presenting himself to two men who were touring the cellar and discussing him at that very moment. They tried to catch him, but their hands passed through him, and the next thing they knew, he was on the other side of the room.

In the early part of this century a visiting minister took it upon himself to exorcize the mischievous ghost of Andreas. It must have worked. Nobody has seen him since. According to the workers there now, he no longer exists.

Lydia's Bridge

Lydia, Still Stuck Under the Bridge

ONE LEGEND, variations of which are common in several areas of the country, originated from the events of one night in Jamestown, North Carolina, during the roaring twenties. This tale has been written and told many times, making it the most well-known Piedmont ghost story, and is retold here because it is such a prominent part of the folklore of the Triad.

Burke Hardison was passing through Jamestown while traveling from Raleigh to High Point late one rainy, dreary night in the spring of 1924. Of course, the thoroughfares in those days were quite a bit different than now, but the small road that would later become U.S. 29-70A was the main artery for a number of routes traversing the center of the state. The road had been a narrow wagon trail for over one hundred years before the dusty path was covered with a macadam surface in 1908. An asphalt surface was put down in 1914. Railroad tracks passed over this road on a wooden bridge, constructed with a slender underpass for the heavy flow of automobiles. That particular night, Burke saw few other cars because of the treacherous weather, and it took all his attention to stay on the pavement. Jamestown was a tiny village that took only a minute to pass through, and he knew the next town he would see after that would be his hometown of High Point.

As Burke slowly approached the railroad underpass, he spotted a lovely young lady in a white evening gown standing beside the road, frantically waving for help. Folks were less suspicious in those days, and Burke pulled over without a second thought. The young lady climbed in, soaking wet from the rain, and said in a dream-like whisper that she was trying to get home to High Point. Since he was heading there already, Burke told her not to worry, that he would get her home safely. She told him the address as they neared the city, but avoided telling him any more information, other than that her name was Lydia. Her soft voice and the fact that she was close to exhaustion accentuated her mystery. Furthermore, Burke could barely hear her due to the heavy rain and the engine noise, as well as the total concentration driving a Model-T in those conditions required. Just before they reached the address she had given him, Burke asked Lydia why she had been standing along the road on such a terrible night, and received the barely audible answer that he should just get her home as soon as possible.

Burke found the address she had given him and stopped in front of the house. Lydia seemed to hesitate, as though she were unable to get out of the car, so Burke got out in the rain and went around to her side to help her to the house. As he opened the car door, he could see the young lady was no longer there. Confused and frightened, Burke went to the front door of the house and knocked, hoping that the girl had jumped out and run inside. A sleepy woman opened the door and looked at him blankly as he told her he had brought Lydia home, but that now she was nowhere to be found. As he waited for an answer from the woman during an uncomfortable silence, Burke shuffled his feet and began to wonder if there really had been anyone in the car with him that night. Tears welled up in the woman's eyes, and she finally explained to him that she had a daughter named Lydia who had looked as he described. Lydia had been returning from a dance in Raleigh a year before during an evening storm, just like the one that night, when she was killed in an automobile accident at the underpass in Jamestown. The woman also said that he was not the first to try to bring her home since then, but Lydia never quite made it all the way. Burke stumbled away, trying to fathom what had happened to him on that night.

This was the first recorded incidence of Lydia catching a ride, although, her mother remarked, there had been others. There are records of the wreck that took her life in 1923, and sightings of Lydia have continued over the years.

The current road was re-routed and the original underpass is a few hundred feet from the graffiti-covered concrete bridge now used, but sightings have also been recorded at the new underpass. In June, 1966, Mr. and Mrs. Frank Fay of Greensboro were driving some friends home to High Point about 11:30 p.m., when Mr. Fay spotted a girl at the underpass. He described her as having long, stringy wet hair. She attempted to flag down the car in front of them, and as the car passed by without stopping, she tried to get in the right door. When Mr. Fay reached the underpass, the girl was gone and he was sure that she had not been able to climb in the car ahead of him. He was so shaken by the incident that he returned home on I-85 that night instead of the route through Jamestown.

There are also numerous incidents of pranks at the underpass. High school students have staged capers, some simple, some elaborate, ranging from placing a student in a white dress alongside the road to using lights to throw ghostly shadows on the underpass. Three boys were caught one night on top of the underpass, dangling a petticoat on a string.

As long as folklore lives, the story of Lydia will remain a favorite. The premature ending of a beautiful young woman's life is made more tragic by the fact that after her death, no matter how hard she tries, she will never be able to get home.

The Haunting of Salem Tavern

THE TAVERN IN OLD SALEM has long been a welcome sight for weary travelers. Today, hungry patrons are served elegant dinners in the old Tavern-Annex building, erected in 1816. The original tavern, rebuilt after a fire in 1784, is next door and houses a museum. Back when people traveled by wagon or horseback, the keeper of the tavern was charged with the important responsibility of providing food, drink, and shelter for the visitors to Salem. Over the years, the keepers did their job well, for the town was famous for its hospitality.

One night long ago, when our country was in its early days, the keeper of the tavern had a visitor who made a lasting impression.

The keeper was working late one September evening around eleven-thirty when he was interrupted by a knock on the front door. Since it was cold and rainy, he figured it was an exhausted traveler hoping to find shelter at that late hour. A man staggered through the door, and looked around with a pale, shriveled face that compelled the keeper to instantly send for the doctor. The traveler collapsed and the keeper helped him to a room to rest.

The doctor arrived and examined the man, but was helpless against the advanced stage of the illness. The man died a few hours later. He had been unable to tell the doctor or

83

tavern keeper his name and there was no identification on his person or in his belongings. He was buried anonymously in the Stranger's Graveyard with a small ceremony, and his belongings were stored in the attic on the slim chance that some member of his family might come by someday to identify them.

The normally smooth operation of the tavern began to fall apart. The servants were on edge, sensing a disturbance in the tavern, and became apprehensive of anything out of order. They had never acted this way before. Their work took twice as long and was of poor quality, and when they refused to go to the basement alone, the keeper demanded to know what the problem was. They told him of strange noises and cold spots in the tavern that had not been there a few days before. The workers claimed the place was being haunted by something.

The tavern keeper first tried to console the servants, then ordered them to stop speaking of such nonsense, but the situation only got worse. One of the men dropped a heavy tray loaded with dishes in the hall, and swore the reason was that something had been following him.

The tavern keeper was in his office one night, looking over his records, when a young maid rushed in and told him that she had seen something horrifying in the attic. She was almost hysterical so the keeper investigated, although he was mostly annoyed. The attic was dark and shadowy, as it always was at night, and he saw nothing out of the ordinary. He started to return to his office, but a sound suddenly caught his ear, a faint, scraping sound. A misty form appeared. Shocked, the keeper's knees began to tremble and he suddenly understood why the maid had been so frightened. He forced himself to look closer at the form, but it was vague and transparent, and impossible for him to make out the facial details. The keeper stood looking at the phantom and wondered if he was in danger, but a soft voice filled the attic, and told the keeper, "You must get word to my fiancée of my death." The voice told him the name of the man who had died

Salem Tavern

a few days ago, and the name of the traveler's lady friend in Charleston, as well as her address. The form vanished, melting into the already eerie shadows. The keeper stood there for a minute and tried to conquer his fear.

After composing himself, the keeper went back to his office, sent the maid back to work, and pulled out his pen. With shaking hands, he wrote a letter to the fiancée in South Carolina, telling of the death of the traveler in the tavern, going into detail about the man and his personal effects which were stored in a wardrobe in the attic.

A few weeks later an elegant young lady arrived by stage coach from South Carolina. She had the deceased man's body transferred from the Stranger's Graveyard to God's Acre, and took possession of his belongings.

As soon as the instructions were carried out, the servants calmed down and everything returned to normal around the tavern. There was no more talk of hauntings. The ghost was apparently satisfied that his belongings were finally in the right hands, and his loved ones were no longer in the dark about his death. The tavern keeper never forgot the incident and related it to friends and acquaintances for the rest of his life.

Editor's Note: Variations of this story have been recorded in several different publications, making it necessary to extract the most common elements from each version in order to depict the story as accurately as possible. A paper by Mary Keene Remsburg, dated August, 1990, was released as *Triad Hauntings* was going to press. Her work, entitled "The Old Salem Legends: The Little Red Man and The Tavern Ghost", suggests that the tavern's ghost may have been Samuel McClary, a Charleston merchant, who died while passing through Salem en route home from Virginia. A tombstone in God's Acre marks McClary's grave and gives the date of his death as September 6, 1831. Ms. Remburg's source for this information is an article in *Old Salem, North Carolina,* a 1941 publication, edited by Mary Barrow Owen.

Miscellaneous Ghosts

Spirits of the Gold Mines

IN DAYS PAST, the gold mines of Guilford County drew men and women of all types, with only one characteristic in common, greed. Two ghostly legends came out of this era.

The Deep River Mine was an active sight before the Civil War. Workers reported that they heard a horrifying scream, followed by a thud at the bottom of the deepest shaft. These noises were heard over and over again. But they were real only once.

Two miners got into a violent argument. No one was ever really sure what started the quarrel, maybe the work, or possession of some gold, or possibly it started over a lady. Whatever the reason, the two men went back to work hating each other. One's hatred was a little stronger than the other's, and when his adversary started down into the shaft, he cut the single rope that supported the miner. The horrible sounds of a man plunging to his death were heard from the shaft, sounds that were repeated by his spirit regularly for several years afterward.

Copper Creek was the sight of the other event that created a legend. In the 1830's, a slave was working in the old rock house, where the ore was brought after mining to be sorted and smelted. An angry supervisor, finding some fault in the slave's work, gave the young man a shove, hard enough to cause the slave to fall through a window. He landed on the jagged rocks below. The slave was killed instantly, his head and body smashed, torn, and bloody. The blood stains that covered the rocks remained long after the slave's body was removed. Though the superintendent is long dead and forgotten, and the rock house is in ruins, the blood on the rocks looks as fresh today as it did the day of the accident one hundred and fifty years ago.

The Gypsy and the Headless Man

ETTA HUFFMAN grew up in a house on old Lexington Road in Winston-Salem back when it was still mostly rural. When she was a twelve year-old girl, about sixty years ago, she tried to help her struggling family make ends meet. Her father came down with a mysterious illness that lingered on for weeks. No medicine helped him recover his energy or get rid of the strange scales that appeared on his arm. One night a gypsy knocked on their door, said she knew about Etta's father's sickness, and offered to help. She also said a woman in the community had placed a spell on him, and that she knew some gypsy charms that could remove the spell. Etta's father was desperate to rid himself of the illness, so he and his wife followed the gypsy back to her camp. Etta was left alone to take care of her two baby brothers.

Etta took the boys on the porch where it was cooler and tried to rock them to sleep. They had just dozed off when Etta felt something like a hand grab her left leg just above the ankle. The porch was built up several feet from the ground, and there were small gaps between the boards, so someone or something could have reached from below her. She was terrified, but sat still and quiet, since she did not want to wake the babies. At last she felt the grip on her leg released, so she quickly stood up and carried the babies inside. It had been too dark on the porch for her to see what had grabbed her. She instantly felt safer on the other side of the screen door.

Etta walked down the hall toward the babies' cribs, but stopped suddenly when she saw something just inside the doorway to her parents' bedroom. Through the dim light she saw a man who wore a navy blue suit, white shirt, and black tie. The man had everything, except a head. He stood facing her, as if he were watching, although he had no eyes.

Etta was petrified. Her discipline prevented her from running or screaming, for that would have awakened the babies. She stumbled down the hall, put the babies to bed, then dashed to her own bed, where she pulled the covers over her head. Etta had never been so happy to see her parents as when they arrived a few minutes later.

The trip to the gypsy's camp apparently worked, for Etta's father almost immediately recovered. They never found any sign of the headless man. The family's lives went back to normal after that, but even after all these years, Etta remembers that night just like it was yesterday.

Jane Aycock

IN THE UPPER REACHES of Aycock Auditorium, on the campus of UNC-Greensboro, an apparition used to float about and scare unsuspecting visitors. The ghost has not been seen for several years and may have left the building for some reason.

Jane Aycock was an eccentric, lonely old woman who lived in a house on Spring Garden Street, precisely where the auditorium now stands. One day she gave up on life, climbed to her attic, and hanged herself.

About sixty years ago, a fine building was erected to display the many outstanding musical and theatrical talents the school produced. Shortly after the opening of the auditorium, the hazy figure of an elderly lady was seen in the balcony area. The ghost of Jane Aycock, the desperately lonely lady during her life, suddenly became a celebrity.

Little has been written or said about the ghost for twenty years. Maybe Jane Aycock tired of the publicity and decided a lonely, quiet life was more to her liking.

The Son Who Couldn't Leave His Mother

THE DEATH of a son or daughter is a tragedy every parent fears. Shirley Beshears went through the pain of losing her nineteen year-old son , Skip, the victim of a hit-and-run driver. He was crossing Highway 158 near Walkertown when a car struck him, killing him instantly.

The days following his death were torturous for Shirley. She found the strength to arrange the funeral, greet hundreds of friends and relatives beside her son's casket, and watch his burial. Her mind constantly questioned why his death had been so meaningless.

The day after the funeral, Shirley sat in her living room and grieved silently. A voice came from behind her, but when she turned she saw no one else in the room. She was amazed when she recognized the voice of her son, Skip. He said, "Please don't cry. Death's not ugly. It's beautiful here." Shirley was stunned for several minutes, but as the words eventually began to sink in, she found comfort in the thought that Skip was content.

Life went on for Shirley. She continued to feel and to see evidence that her son was somehow nearby. Lights in her house went on and off for no reason, except that they seemed to follow the habits of Skip when he had been alive. Shirley and her neighbor were lying in the sun one day beside her son's car, which still sat in the yard. The door on the driver's side suddenly opened, though no one had touched it.

Shirley and her friend, Margie, were driving to the store one night along Highway 158, when they passed a pedestrian that they both recognized as Skip. Shirley slammed on the brakes, turned around, and went back, but there was no pedestrian anywhere in sight.

Skip's tragic death still haunts Shirley, but she knows he is all right in his other world, and that his spirit is watching and willing to communicate with her whenever she grieves.

The Haunted Sewing Machine

A LADY named Jeannie (not her real name), who now lives near King, rented a house in High Point a little over twenty years ago. She and her husband moved their belongings into the quaint, old house, located just off Kivett Drive. Since they were a struggling young family with two small children, Jeannie took a job during the day while her husband worked at night. That way they saved the expense of a baby-sitter.

The family had few possessions and almost no furniture, so they were pleased to find in one of the rooms an old sewing machine, stored in a beautiful cherry-wood cabinet. Although Jeannie was unable to get the sewing machine to work, the cabinet was a handsome piece of furniture for their living room. She placed a small lamp on top of it.

Alone with the children one night, Jeannie was startled to hear the sound of a sewing machine inside the house. She ran into the living room, whereupon the noise stopped. There was no one there and the cabinet and lamp were sitting undisturbed. Jeannie left the room, and a few minutes later she heard the sounds again. When she investigated, again the noise ceased and everything looked normal.

Jeannie later went to bed and once again heard the strange sounds. This time she did not go to investigate. The sewing machine started and stopped over and over, ran at different speeds, and sounded as though some garment were being stitched together. She even heard a click that sounded like a bobbin being replaced, then several seconds of silence as though the thread was being slipped through the needle, followed by the motor noise from the sewing machine. The sounds lasted about twenty minutes before they stopped for the night.

The same events began to happen on a regular basis. Jeannie was afraid to stay in the house at night without her husband, and talked her sister from Durham into spending some time with her. The first night her sister was there, the house was quiet all evening. The second night, Jeannie said she heard something, but it turned out to be a truck passing by outside. Her sister agreed to stay one more night before going home.

That night as Jeannie and her sister went to bed, they both felt apprehensive. A few minutes later, they heard the sound of the sewing machine. It started slowly, then picked up speed. The two women tip-toed down the hall toward the living room, where the noise was undeniably originating. Just before they reached the entrance, the sounds stopped, and when they entered the living room all seemed normal. Jeannie's sister insisted on a thorough search of the room, so they looked carefully inside the cabinet at the sewing machine, under the two chairs and end table that were there, and at the mantel over the fireplace. They found nothing out of the ordinary. The two ladies looked through the window and saw nothing. Then they noticed their reflections in the window pane from the dim light cast by the lamp on the cabinet. Both of their mouths dropped open when they realized, at exactly the same instant, that there were three faces reflected on the glass!

Jeannie and her sister both screamed and tore through the house, grabbed the children and the keys to her sister's car, and ran outside. They jumped into the car and started down the street, but the engine went dead before they had gone a block, and they coasted into a deserted parking lot. When the car refused to start again, they sat there silently and stared at each other. With nowhere to go, they spent the night sitting in the parking lot.

Jeannie and her husband moved out of the house a week later. When the landlord asked them why they were moving, Jeannie told him that she was allergic to something in the house. He had been so nice to them that she didn't have the heart to tell him the house was haunted.

All Jeannie can remember about the third face in the window was that it was female, and it was smiling. Who this phantom seamstress was, and if she still resides in the house, are two questions we can't answer.

Unrequited Love

THE YOUNG WOMEN who reside in Clewell Dormitory on the campus of Salem College know the story of the Clewell ghost, and when they lose in love, it is their scapegoat.

As legend has it, the ghost is the spirit of a young former student of Salem, who attended the school many years ago.

Before she left home for school, her parents procured a mate for her, an older man whom she didn't love at all, but who would provide security for her. With her fate sealed, her parents packed her off to finishing school at Salem to prepare her to be a genteel wife. Like most women of the time, she accepted her parents' decision.

She moved into Clewell, and began her studies in home economics, but soon she met a handsome young man who lived nearby. They fell deeply in love, and when her parents found out, they ordered her home immediately. Deeply depressed and torn, the young woman climbed into the attic and hanged herself.

Now, many of Clewell's residents say her spirit sets out to sabotage the loves of the present day tenants. There are rumors her apparition roams the halls, weeping.

Clewell Dormitory

← BC

NCB